A Present From Earth

For Eleanor Huggins-Cooper

Find out more about **Ricky Rocket** at
www.shoo-rayner.co.uk

ORCHARD BOOKS
338 Euston Road, London NW1 3BH
Orchard Books Australia
Hachette Children's Books
Level 17/207 Kent St, Sydney, NSW 2000

ISBN 978 1 84616 389 0 (paperback)

First published in Great Britain in 2006
First paperback publication in 2007

Text and illustrations © Shoo Rayner 2006

1 3 5 7 9 10 8 6 4 2 (hardback)
3 5 7 9 10 8 6 4 2 (paperback)

Printed in Great Britain

A Present From Earth

Shoo Rayner

ORCHARD BOOKS

Ricky Rocket stuck his feet out of the cupboard under the stairs and waggled them.

Ricky is the only Earth boy on the planet of Hammerhead and his little sister, Sue, is the only Earth girl on the planet.

4

"Hickle, hickle!" Sue giggled, as she crept up and tickled Ricky's pink, wriggling toes.

Ricky jerked and hit his head
on a shelf.

Ricky whooshed up
the stairs after his
sister. "Wait till I get
you, you little…"

The air filled with the kind
of ear-splitting, blood-curdling,
brain-jamming scream that
little Earth girls are famous for
all over the universe.

Mum blocked the landing and shouted over the din. "What's going on?"

"Ricky's chasing me!" Sue whined.

"She started it!" Ricky complained. "She made me hit my head in the cupboard."

"What were you doing in there?"
Mum asked.

"I've got to find something from Earth for show-and-tell day tomorrow," Ricky explained.

"Oh Ricky!" Mum sighed, deeply. "It's nearly bedtime. Why do you always leave things to the last minute?"

"You're in trouble!" Sue sing-songed.

Ricky lunged at his sister, but Mum caught him by the collar and held him back, like an attack dog on a short lead.

Mum took a deep breath. "Sue...go and get ready for bed! Ricky...tell me exactly what you need for this show-and-tell day."

FIVE HORRIBLE THINGS ABOUT LITTLE SISTERS
They smell!
They scream!
They tell tales
They play with dolls!
They're GURLS!

Ricky Rocket's classmates came from all over the universe, so show-and-tell days were always interesting and often quite dangerous. Most of the things Ricky wanted to take to school were now banned!

Ricky told Mum about the day his best friend, Bubbles, had brought some music from the planet Fuddleduddle.

"Listen to this!" Bubbles enthused. The music was dreamy. It sounded like tinkly silver bubbles floating in the air.

"It's so beautiful," the Rogan sisters trilled, before they fell into a deep trance. They didn't wake up again until the end of term, so music had been banned from show-and-tell days.

MUSIC FROM THE PLANET FUDDLEDUDDLE

Played on **fudPods** – half-plant, half-machine.

fudPods live in bowls of water with special **fud** food.

Put together, they **"sing"** wonderful harmonies about the beauty of the universe.

Some people say they sound like a herd of cows **mooing** in tune.

There was only one thing Ricky didn't like about school…Grip. Grip was the biggest and ugliest creature in the class.

Grip came from Hammerhead, so he thought he was in charge. On his show-and-tell day, he showed them a game called shark hunt.

Grip hid a small, stone shark's head under one of three cups, which were placed upside down on the table. Grip muddled up the cups and you had to guess where the shark was.

It looked easy, but however carefully Ricky watched he could never choose the cup with the shark!

"I'll do it r-e-e-e-ally slo-o-o-wly,"
Grip smirked. "Watch very closely."
Ricky never took his eyes off the cup
that hid the shark's head. He was
positive he knew which cup to choose.

"It's definitely under that one," he
said, pointing to the cup nearest to him.

Grip smiled an oily, toothy smile.
"Want to bet?"

Their class teacher Mizz Fizz
bleeped excitedly. Red and green
lights flashed on her head as her
electronic brain worked out the maths
of Grip's game.

"I would say," she finally announced,
"that there a is ninety-nine point nine,
nine, nine percent chance of Ricky's
choice being correct!"

Ricky tingled all over. He was so
sure he was right, he bet his best
Lord Vorg game card on it.

Grip leered as he pulled the cup away.
"I don't believe it!" Ricky gasped.
"It's not there! It must be a trick!"

By dinnertime, Grip had won Grombolian marbles, upside-down pens, tiddly-winx and all sorts of other stuff off his classmates.

Mizz Fizz had bet and lost fifteen good behaviour stars...those were the first stars Grip had ever had!

Eventually, Mister Blister, the headteacher, proved that the game was a trick and made Grip give back everything he had won. He banned games from show-and-tell days.

Tammy Tweetle showed her pet Blooba from the planet Twizzle. Blooba are a sort of cuddly, flying plant.

"It's so cute!" Ricky said. He opened the cage when Tammy wasn't looking.

DON'T LET IT OUT!

Tammy shrieked with an ear-splitting, blood-curdling, brain-jamming scream. Ricky thought only little Earth girls could scream like that!

Too late! The Blooba squawked and shot out of the cage. It landed on Dooley's furry head. The Blooba immediately began growing roots in Dooley's hair.

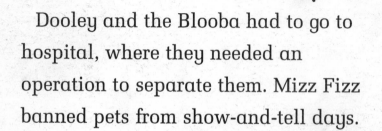

Dooley and the Blooba had to go to hospital, where they needed an operation to separate them. Mizz Fizz banned pets from show-and-tell days.

WEIRD SPACE PLANTS

Amoebids
Swallow raw
like oysters to help
digest heavy meals.

Transmitter lilies

Can send messages
across deep space.

Sweet Neptune
Only sweet if you
come from Neptune. The
smelliest flower in
the universe – don't be
taken in by the smiley face!

Callisto Cabbage
Grows wild in the
stinkbogs of Callisto.

Little known fact:
Super Nova candyfloss is made from Callisto Cabbage.

Mum and Ricky searched for
Earth things that he could show
and talk about.

"How about Sue's doll's house
furniture?" Mum suggested. "They're
like models of Earth things."

"He's not having anything of mine!"
Sue yelled from her room.

"I wouldn't take any of your stupid,
girly things!" Ricky snapped back.

"What about this old alarm clock?"
Mum soothed. "It's got Earth hours.
That's really interesting."

"B-o-o-o-ring!" Ricky groaned.

Mum held up an Earth cookery book.
There was a picture of a tasty chicken
casserole on the cover. "How about this?"

"Roosta wouldn't like it," Ricky
explained. "She's a chicken person!"

Mum sighed. "We've moved around the universe so often, we haven't got much stuff left that actually comes from Earth."

Ricky hadn't been to Earth since he was a tiny baby. He had nothing to show, and not much to tell.

The next morning, at breakfast, Ricky was in a gloomy mood. He was thinking up excuses to tell Mizz Fizz, when the Postbot rang the bell and delivered a huge parcel.

The Rocket Family
10572 Infinite Loop
Hammerhead
Crab Nebula

"It's from Granny Earth." Dad said, as he cut through the shrink-wrapper. "I wonder what she's sent us?"

"Winterval presents!" Ricky and Sue cheered. There were presents for all of them, wrapped in colourful paper with pictures of little red birds and houses covered in snow.

There was a box of candles for
Candlenight and...two bars of chocolate.

"Mmmm...chocolate. My favourite!"
Ricky sighed. Then a bright idea
struck him. "I'll take the chocolate to
school. That's one Earth thing I can
talk about for hours!"

WINTERVAL

Before global warming in the 21st century, Earthlings used to brighten up the winter season with many festivals.
These are all now remembered at **WINTERVAL**.

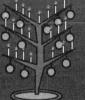

Trees are decorated with electric candles and silver balls.

Presents like socks or candy are given.

Candles are lit in the window to welcome family and visitors.

When Mizz Fizz called Ricky to the front of the class, he was ready.

"This is chocolate," he explained, holding up the purple and silver package. "It's made from cocoa seeds. It melts on your tongue in the most wonderful warm, sweet, gooey way. It is probably the most favourite thing on Earth."

"Let's have a bit then!" said Grip.

Ricky's heart missed a beat. He hadn't thought that he might have to share his precious chocolate. Sue would never share hers!

"Well, Ricky?" Mizz Fizz asked. "Can we try some of your chocolate?"

Ricky knew it would be rude to say no. "Oh! Err! Yes, Mizz…" he stammered. "I–I suppose so."

Reluctantly, he slid a finger under the shiny, purple wrapper and flipped it open. Then, slowly, he unpeeled the silver paper. He broke the chocolate up into squares and, with a sinking heart, offered them to his classmates.

Shelby took the silver paper and ate it! "Mmm! Quite good," he said. "Not as good as the stuff we get on my planet."

"No!" Ricky explained. "The brown stuff is the chocolate. Just stick it in your mouth and let it melt."

Some of Ricky's classmates were cold-blooded. The chocolate wouldn't melt in their mouths, so they crunched at it.

"Mmm, it's sort of like eating soft beetles," said Dooley.

"It don't taste of nuthin'," Grip growled, as he swallowed his piece in one go.

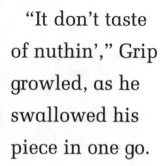

Bubbles was so warm-blooded that the chocolate melted too quickly and dribbled from the corner of his mouth.

FRRRRRP!

FRRRRRP!

The trumpets on Bubbles' head were making the most extraordinary sounds.

Brown, chocolatey
bubbles began oozing
from his trumpets
and floated around
the room.

FRRRRRRP!

All around him, Ricky's classmates clutched their stomachs and groaned.

Terrible burping and burbling noises filled the room. There was a horrible, sweet, chocolatey stink in the air.

Then, as if someone had given a signal, twenty-five assorted aliens made a stampede for the door.

Luckily the school had lots of different toilets – at least one for every kind of alien in the school – so there weren't any major accidents.

Ricky felt fine, of course. Mizz Fizz
called for a doctor. Ricky watched the
doctor put the last few crumbs of his
chocolate into an analyser.

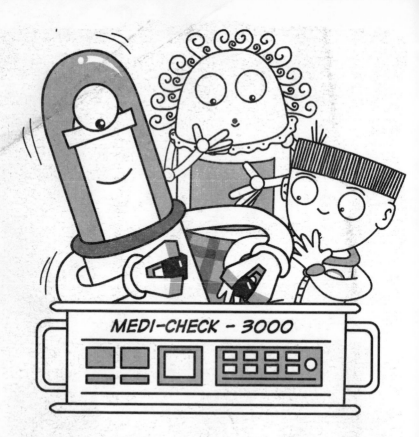

MEDI-CHECK - 3000

"Ah!" the doctor smiled. "This chocolate stuff of yours contains methylxanthines, the most powerful laxative known in the universe. Anyone who eats chocolate, except for Earthlings, of course, will need to go to the toilet faster than a shooting star!"

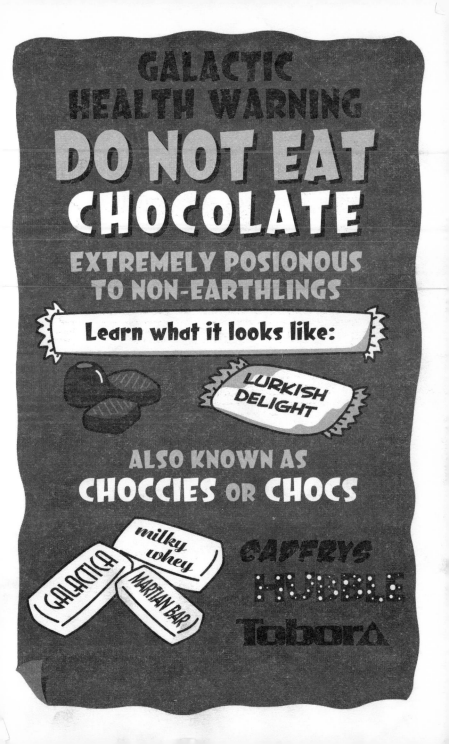

After school, Mum chatted with
Mizz Fizz. "How was Ricky's
show-and-tell?" she asked.

"Well…" Mizz Fizz flashed some
purple lights. "Ricky made quite
an impression on the class!"

Mum gave Ricky a hug. "Oh well
done, Ricky!"

Ricky stared at his feet. Mum would hear the truth in the end.

"So everyone liked his talk then?" Mum asked.

Mizz Fizz's light twinkled from purple to red. "I think we can say that Ricky has taught us everything we'll ever need to know about chocolate!"

Ricky Rocket

Shoo Rayner

Enjoy all these Ricky Rocket stories!